WILDCATS

BLITZ

BY JAKE MADDOX

ILLUSTRATED BY SEAN TIFFANY

WILDCATS FOOTBA[LL]

LE HUSKIES

CYCLONES

HALES

LIONS

CCANEERS

ES

ES

ARS

IS

CANEERS

Published by Stone Arch Books
A Capstone Imprint
151 Good Counsel Drive, P.O. Box 669
Mankato, Minnesota 56002
www.capstonepub.com

First published in 2011 by Stone Arch Books as:
Quarterback Comeback
Linebacker Block
Speed Receiver
Running Back Dreams

Library of Congress Cataloging-in-Publication Data is available on
the Library of Congress website.

ISBN: 978-1-4342-2887-1
Summary: Four stories about the Wildcats football team.
Photo Credits: ShutterStock/Mike Flippo (p. 6, 7, 56, 57, 106, 107, 158, 159)

TABLE OF CONTENTS

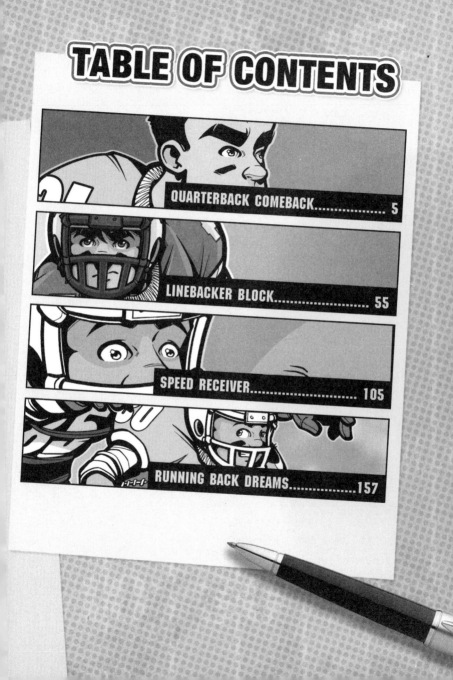

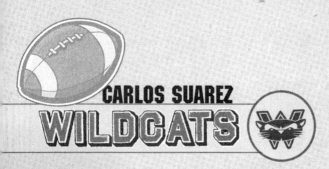

CARLOS SUAREZ

WILDCATS

TABLE OF CONTENTS

CHAPTER 1

IMPROVISED

It was Thursday afternoon. At Westfield Junior High, the eighth-grade Wildcats football team was having practice.

Carlos Suarez, the star quarterback, crouched five yards behind his center for a shotgun snap. "Hut!" he shouted. "Hut!"

After a pause, the center snapped the ball. Carlos caught it and turned to his right. The running back came around him for the handoff.

"It was supposed to be a long play," Andrew said. He pulled off his helmet. Carlos could tell his teammate was angry.

The coach nodded. "Yes, it was," he said. "But the defense was tight on the receivers. Carlos improvised. It was a smart move, and it worked."

Carlos smiled. "Right," he said. "I saw the best move would be to run the ball myself."

Andrew crossed his arms. "Next time, I'll get open," he said. Carlos could tell that Andrew wasn't happy with what had happened. Carlos seemed like a champion, while Andrew had failed in his role as receiver.

The coach blew his whistle. "Okay, everyone," he said. "That's it for practice. We've got a big game tomorrow, so go home and rest up."

"Against the Huskies," Logan Meltzer said.

Logan was new to Westfield. He had just moved from River City. Now he was the Wildcats' starting middle linebacker.

"They're pretty tough," Logan went on. "There are some seriously strong guys on that team."

Carlos laughed. Logan was one of the strongest guys on the Wildcats. Carlos thought it was really funny to hear him call other players "seriously strong."

"Logan's right," Coach French said. "They are tough. But you guys know that Westfield has a history against the Huskies. As some of you know, the eighth-grade Wildcats football team has never defeated the eighth-grade Huskies."

Carlos smirked. "We can get them this year, Coach," he said. "I'm the quarterback, so they don't stand a chance!"

Andrew rolled his eyes, and Logan laughed.

Coach French turned to Carlos. "You're one of the best QBs we've had, Carlos," he said. "But you're not invincible."

"I'm super quick, Coach," Carlos said. He ran in place and did a few dodges. Some other guys on the team laughed.

The coach shook his head. "These guys are big and fast," Coach said. "You might find running the ball or relying on the short game will be tougher than normal."

Carlos smiled. "They won't be able to catch me," he said. "This will be a piece of cake."

Coach French looked at Carlos for a long moment.

"I hope you're right, Carlos," Coach French said. "You'll be calling the plays in the game. Remember to keep your options open, just like you did in practice today. Okay?"

Carlos shrugged. "Sure, Coach," he said.

Coach French shook his head again. Then he looked at the rest of the team. "Okay, boys," he said. "Hit the showers and then head home to rest up for the big game."

He clapped once and patted Andrew on the back. Then the team headed to the locker room.

CHAPTER 2

GAME DAY

The next day was the big game against the Huskies. After their last class, Andrew and Carlos walked together to the locker room. The halls were crowded with people hurrying home for the weekend.

Carlos was all smiles, thinking about the game against the Huskies. He wasn't at all nervous about the game. But Andrew was worried because of what Logan and Coach French had said. "You heard the coach," Andrew said. "And that new kid, Logan. The Huskies are tough, Carlos!"

"And I'm tough too," Carlos replied. He held out his arm and flexed. "Not to mention fast, smart, and smooth. Those guys don't stand a chance with me as QB."

"I think we should try some of those passing plays we've been practicing," Andrew said. "Passing might be key against the Huskies."

Soon they were at the locker room. Carlos pushed the doors open. Most of their teammates were already there, getting into their uniforms.

"Listen, Andrew," Carlos said. "Coach French wants me to call the plays. I think the short game is going to be the way to go today."

"I hope you're right," Andrew said. He pulled his shoes out of his locker. "Because I don't want Westfield to lose to the Huskies again this year."

Carlos pulled off his sweater and shoved it in his locker. "Quit worrying, will you?" he said. "It's going to be fine."

CHAPTER 3

LOVE OF THE GAME

The game against the Huskies started at four. It was early for Friday night football, but the high school team's game would start at seven. The eighth-grade game needed to be over before then.

Carlos was the first person out on the field. He liked to get out first to take it all in. Since it was a Friday, the grounds crew had been out that day, mowing the field and repainting all the yard lines. Carlos loved the smell of the fresh-cut grass. He loved how bright and white the new yard lines were. But he didn't love anything more than the feel of a football in his hands.

Sometimes, he loved that feeling so much, he didn't want to pass the ball or hand it off. He just wanted to keep it and run for the end zone.

While Carlos threw the ball around by himself, the rest of the Wildcats showed up at the field. Soon, the Huskies' bus arrived in the parking lot.

Carlos watched as the other team marched to their bench. The Huskies uniform was silver and white, with black numbers. Their helmets were silver, too, with a picture of a black dog, howling.

The game would be starting soon. Carlos took a deep breath and headed over to his team's bench. As quarterback, he felt the pressure of this game. He knew it was up to him to end their losing streak against the Huskies.

Before the game-opening kickoff, Coach French gathered everyone in a huddle by the bench. "All right, everyone," he said. "Let's look alive out there. Remember, Carlos will be calling most of the plays."

Andrew looked at Carlos. Carlos tried to ignore his teammate's stare.

The coach went on. "Carlos, we all know you're strong in the short game," he said. "But remember, if you need to pass, pass."

"I know, Coach," Carlos said. Then he smiled and added, "But I really doubt I'll need to."

Coach patted him on the shoulder. "Okay," he said, "on three, break. One, two, three . . ."

"Break!" the whole team shouted. The kickoff-return team ran out to the field.

Andrew caught the kickoff at the ten-yard line. He cut toward the sideline, then dodged back toward the center. After losing two Huskies, he was finally tackled at the forty.

Carlos gave Andrew a high five. "Good run," Carlos said. "Now let's see what I can do with it."

Logan rolled his eyes and sat on the bench. Andrew and Carlos headed out to the forty-yard line for first down.

In the huddle, Carlos called a handoff to the running back, Kyle Aaronson. Then Carlos clapped. Everyone shouted, "Break!"

Carlos took the snap at shotgun. Then he spun right and handed the ball off to Kyle.

Kyle came around to the left side behind the line. Then he started running up the sideline as fast as he could. But he wasn't quick or big enough to get past the Huskies linebackers.

Kyle was knocked out of bounds. He hadn't even crossed the scrimmage line.

"Loss of three yards," the referee called after blowing his whistle. "Wildcats on the thirty-seven. Second down!"

Carlos shook his head. "You have to shake those guys, Kyle!" he said when the team was back in the huddle. "Okay, let's try the same thing, other way, but play action. I'll run it through the middle when the linebackers come after you, Kyle. Everyone got it?"

When everyone nodded, Carlos said, "Okay, break!"

Carlos got into shotgun again. "Hut!" he yelled.

The Huskies middle linebacker laughed. "Are these guys doing another handoff?" he said.

Carlos took the snap and spun to his left. He faked the handoff to Kyle.

But it didn't work. Soon every Huskies player was chasing Carlos. He never even got across the line of scrimmage.

The referee blew his whistle. "Loss of two yards," he said. "Third down, Wildcats ball."

Andrew helped Carlos up. "This is a pretty slow short game we're playing right now," he said.

Carlos shook him off. "Don't worry about it," he said. "We're softening them up. It's still early."

Everyone headed back to the huddle. Andrew slowly joined them. "I hope you're right," he mumbled to Carlos. "I really hope you're right."

CHAPTER 4

LOSING

Toward the end of the first quarter, the score was still 0-0. After a Huskies punt to the forty-five, it took the Wildcats two downs to get the ball to the fifty.

In the huddle before third down, Carlos called the first Wildcats passing play. "Let's try a screen to Kyle out to the right," Carlos said. "Play action, I'll roll left and then throw to you, Kyle. You should be wide open if I can keep them on me."

"Okay," Kyle said, but he sounded worried. He hadn't gotten more than a yard or so against the Huskies yet. They were just too tough.

"Okay, break," Carlos said. He was starting to sound tired.

Carlos took the snap from shotgun again. He rolled to the left and faked the handoff to Kyle.

The Huskies middle linebacker shouted, "Play action!"

Carlos had been hoping they'd spot the fake, though. He ran to the left sideline and immediately turned and threw the screen pass to Kyle.

But Carlos hadn't been quick enough. The Huskies defensive line was on Kyle in an instant.

Kyle fell at the scrimmage line for no gain. Carlos hurried to the huddle.

"Are we going for it, Carlos?" Kyle asked when the huddle was together again.

Carlos shook his head. "Nope. It's way too risky," he said.

"A quick pass over top and we can get the five we need for first down," Andrew said.

Carlos thought a second. Then he shook his head. "No, that's too risky too," he said. "We'll punt."

Carlos waved to the sidelines, and the punting team came in.

It was a good punt, and the Huskies started on the ten-yard line. The Huskies running game was strong, though, and they converted for two first downs.

Soon, they were in range for a touchdown.

"Come on, defense!" Coach French called out. "Force the field goal!"

But the Huskies offense was too tough. Logan did his best to get to their quarterback, but he was too late. The Huskies completed a pass right in the end zone for the touchdown to end the first quarter.

Everyone on the bench moaned.

"That's okay," Andrew said. "That was only one quarter. We can easily come back."

But not one person on the team looked sure.

CHAPTER 5

THE SECOND QUARTER

The referee called the players on for the start of the second quarter. Carlos started to head for the field, but Coach French grabbed his arm.

"Are you still confident in the short game, Carlos?" Coach French asked.

Carlos nodded. "They're starting to soften in the middle," he said. "We can pull this out."

The coach sighed, then patted Carlos on the back. "Okay, Carlos," he said. "I'm trusting you because you're my star quarterback. But you'll have to prove you can call these plays."

"Got it," Carlos said.

After the kickoff, Carlos went out to the huddle for the first Wildcats possession of the second quarter.

The pressure's really on now, he thought. *I have to stop relying on Kyle.*

The rest of the offense waited for him in the huddle.

You know the old saying, he thought. *If you want something done right, you have to do it all by yourself.*

Carlos reached the huddle. "I'm going to run it myself," he said. "Break."

The other players looked at each other as Carlos got into shotgun position.

"Hut," Carlos said. "Hut!" He caught the snap. He quickly faked left toward Kyle and then ran beside Kyle toward the right side. The defensive line followed them.

Carlos started running upfield, and Kyle threw one block. It let Carlos make it past the line of scrimmage for a gain of five yards.

Carlos jogged back to the huddle. "Same again," he said quickly. "Break!"

The Wildcats ran the same exact play, and the Huskies didn't expect it. Carlos gained eight yards on the run. The Wildcats had their first conversion of the game.

Back in the huddle, Carlos looked at Kyle. "Great blocks," Carlos said. "This time we go left. Break!" Carlos said.

As the team lined up, Andrew went over to Kyle. "Why does Carlos think you're the only players on the team?" Andrew asked.

Kyle just shrugged. "I don't know," he said. "I'm not the one calling the plays."

Carlos caught the snap. Kyle came up behind him and turned around. Then the two of them ran toward the left sideline.

The Huskies line had had enough, though. They rushed through the blockers and tackled Carlos ten yards behind the line of scrimmage.

Carlos got to his feet and threw down the football. "Man!" he shouted as the ball bounced on the field.

The referee blew his whistle. "Second down, Wildcats ball," he said.

Then the ref said quietly to Carlos, "Watch that temper, quarterback. Okay?"

"Sorry," Carlos said, but he couldn't help being upset.

The next two downs didn't go well either. Carlos tried running again and got nowhere. On third down, he tried a screen pass to Kyle, but it was incomplete.

"Are we punting?" Kyle asked.

Carlos shook his head. "No way," he said. "I'm not giving up now."

"Carlos!" Coach French called out. "Why aren't you calling in the special team?"

Carlos ignored him.

"I'm taking it up the middle," Carlos said. "I need excellent blocking."

He looked at his offensive line. "Don't fail me, okay?" he said.

Everyone in the line grunted, but it seemed impossible to run twenty yards against the Huskies.

Carlos called, "Break!" The team got into a tight-snap formation.

Carlos took the snap, and the line tightened around him to block. Carlos managed to push through the crowd of offense and defense for a gain of seven yards, but it wasn't nearly enough.

CHAPTER 6

BIG TROUBLE

Carlos got up and angrily pulled off his helmet. But he wasn't the only angry person on the field.

Andrew glared at Carlos, and Coach French was steaming at the bench, pacing back and forth. Carlos groaned.

"You should have called for the punt, Carlos," Andrew said, walking over to Carlos. "You need to stop hotdogging out there."

"Who's hotdogging?" Carlos replied. He got right up in Andrew's face. "You just can't ever get open."

"Whatever," Andrew said, turning away. "If you keep trying to make every play by yourself, we'll never score. We'll lose the game, and it'll be your fault." Then Andrew quickly walked over to the bench and sat down.

Carlos headed to the bench too. Coach French was waiting to talk to him.

"Carlos!" the coach snapped. "What happened out there? Why didn't you call the punt? That was an impossible first down."

Carlos sheepishly looked down, frowning. "I thought I could make it," he said. Then he threw his helmet down and sat on the bench to watch the Huskies' possession.

The Huskies were on the Wildcats' forty-yard line, and the first half was almost over. After the snap, the Huskies quarterback rolled out right. He had all the time he needed to let his receivers get open. His offensive linemen were just too big and fast to get past.

Finally he launched the ball twenty-five yards. The Wildcats tackled the receiver right away, but it was a big gain and first down.

On the next play, the Huskies quarterback made a play action pass right up the middle for a short gain. But they didn't need a very big gain.

Going into second down, the Huskies were only ten yards from the end zone and another seven points.

"Look alive out there, defense!" Coach French shouted. Carlos watched from the bench.

On second down, the Huskies running back took a handoff up the right side. Logan got a hand on him at the line for a tackle. The Huskies were only one yard from another TD. "Third down, on the one," the referee called out.

The Huskies came out of their huddle and lined up. "Hut!" the Huskies quarterback said. "Hut!" And the center snapped the ball.

The Huskies quarterback, who looked just as big as the rest of his team, launched himself right over the line for a quarterback sneak. It was another touchdown for the Huskies. After the extra point, it was 14-0 at halftime.

CHAPTER 7

HALFTIME

The Wildcats gathered on the benches in the locker room during halftime. Coach French looked at the ground and shook his head. Andrew glared at Carlos. The whole team looked upset. Everyone sat on the benches, slouched over, with their heads hanging low. Carlos felt like a complete loser.

"Well, that was a rough first half," the coach said. "If we don't change our strategy, we don't stand a chance."

"That's what I've been saying," Andrew said under his breath.

"I don't get it!" Carlos said. He stood up. "Why isn't the running game working? It always works for us."

"No plan ever works all the time, Carlos," Coach French replied. "Sometimes you have to change your plan."

"Obviously, this is one of those times," Logan said with a chuckle. A few other guys laughed.

"I don't know," Carlos said.

"If you're going to be a good quarterback, and not just a superstar," the coach said, "you have to be able to use your teammates' strengths, not just your own."

"What do you mean?" Carlos asked.

"I mean, look for Andrew out there, for example," the coach replied. "This is a team, and everyone has his own skills. We have the players for a great passing game."

"Yeah," Andrew added, "if you think you can connect."

"Hey!" Carlos shot back. "I'll have no problem finding you if you can get open."

"Oh, I'll get open," Andrew replied. He jumped to his feet and stared Carlos down.

"Okay, guys," Coach French said. "Save that attitude for the field."

"Everyone huddle up," Carlos said. "On three, teamwork," Carlos said. He glanced at Coach French. The coach smiled and joined the huddle. "One, two, three . . ."

"Teamwork!"

CHAPTER 8

PASSING GAME

The second half opened with a Wildcats kickoff. The Huskies returned the ball to their own thirty-yard line.

On the Huskies' first down, they managed to gain three yards on a handoff.

"That's all right," Coach French shouted. "Hold them there."

The Wildcats defense was feeling good. When the Huskies snapped again, they rushed. The quarterback went down behind the line, for a loss of three yards.

On third down, the Huskies tried for a short pass to convert, but it was incomplete. They were forced to punt.

Andrew returned the punt to midfield, and the Wildcats offense took the field.

In the huddle, Carlos pointed at Kyle. "Handoff," Carlos said.

"What?" Andrew snapped. "After what the coach just said?"

"Trust me," Carlos replied. "Break!"

Carlos took the snap and went to handoff to Kyle. But he faked the handoff and ran left. The Huskies line took him down with a one-yard loss.

"This quarterback is a joke," the Huskies middle linebacker shouted. "He just keeps trying to run. Doesn't he see he can't get past us?"

The other Huskies linebackers grunted and bumped helmets. Carlos could tell they were feeling pretty confident.

In the huddle, Carlos turned to Andrew.

"Play action, I'll roll out and find you," Carlos said. "Get open, and cut across midfield, okay?"

Andrew nodded, and Carlos said, "Break!"

Carlos took the snap in shotgun. He rolled to his left and faked the handoff to Kyle. Kyle bolted for the right as Carlos rolled out to the left.

"Play action!" the Huskies linebacker shouted. The defense came at Carlos as he scanned upfield for Andrew.

As he looked, Andrew faked long and cut left toward the middle of the field. Carlos pulled back and launched a perfect spiral up the middle.

Andrew's defender was left in the dust as the wide receiver caught the pass. He turned up field and ran easily.

Touchdown!

CHAPTER 9

TEN POINTS DOWN

The Wildcats kicked the extra point to make the score 14-7. On the kickoff, the Huskies ran up to their own forty-yard line.

The Wildcats defense took the field.

The Huskies were angry now. They hadn't wanted to give up even one point. So far, the second half wasn't going so well.

The Huskies quarterback shouted the signals from shotgun formation.

The center snapped the ball. The quarterback spun out to the left and handed off to their running back.

Logan tried to get to him, but wasn't quick enough. The Huskies running back almost made it to the fifty before the Wildcats defense could get him down.

On second down, the quarterback took a tight snap. He connected with a short pass right over the line. The receiver ran the ball all the way to the thirty. It was first down.

The Huskies were feeling better now. They were within field goal range, and it was first down. The Huskies quarterback took the snap and faked handoff. He rolled out to the right and passed. It was incomplete. The Huskies quarterback shook his head and went back to the huddle.

On second down, the Huskies went for another pass. But the Wildcats defense knocked the pass to the ground for another incomplete.

The Huskies were still ten yards from a first down. If they didn't make it this time, they would have to kick the field goal.

"Break!" the Huskies quarterback shouted. They lined up in shotgun formation.

"Hut!" the quarterback called. "Hike!"

He caught the snap and handed off to the running back. The back ran for the right side and cut up the field.

Logan was on him right away. The Huskies running back was down at the twenty-eight.

"Good job, D," Coach French called out.

The Huskies kicking team came in for the field goal. After the snap, the Wildcats defense pushed into the line and jumped, trying to block the kick. But the ball sailed over them and went through the uprights.

The Huskies made the field goal to bring the score to 17-7. The Wildcats would still need to score twice to take the lead or even tie up the game. They only had the fourth quarter left.

CHAPTER 10

TWO-MINUTE WARNING

With two minutes left, the Wildcats were still down by ten points. It was third down, and they were on the fifty.

"Okay, Andrew," Carlos said. "Let's go for that long pass. Play action, and I'll hit you at the sideline at their twenty-five. You take it home."

"Will do," Andrew said, smiling.

Carlos took the snap and spun to his right. Kyle came around behind him for the fake handoff.

The Huskies line shifted to follow Kyle as Carlos ran fast toward the sideline and found Andrew.

He pulled back and launched the ball straight up the sidelines as Andrew cut to lose his defender. It was good!

Andrew darted up the field. His defender couldn't keep up. Andrew crossed the line. Another touchdown! But it wasn't over yet.

Coach French called the team to the bench. "We're still down by three, boys," the coach said. "Hold them tight on defense. Then, if we can get close enough, let's get the field goal and finish these Huskies off in overtime."

The Huskies returned the kickoff to the forty. On their first offensive play, though, Logan burst through the line and sacked their quarterback. He fumbled the ball, and Logan scooped it up.

The entire Huskies offensive line was on top of him instantly, but the Wildcats had possession at the Huskies' twenty-five. Now it was up to Carlos and the offense to score. But there was only time for one play!

CHAPTER 11

ONE LAST PLAY

The offense took the field. Carlos called everyone into the huddle. "Okay, guys," Carlos said. "In the second half, we've been using the passing game, and it's been great."

Andrew smiled. "That's right," he said.

"Now, we need only twenty-five yards, and they'll be expecting us to pass," Carlos went on.

"Aren't we going to pass?" Kyle asked.

Carlos looked at Andrew, then over at Kyle. "I think now is the time for me to go back to my skills, guys," Carlos said. "I need to do what I do best. Here's the plan."

Carlos filled the team in on his plan. Then they took the field.

When play began, Carlos took the snap in shotgun position. He spun to his left, where Kyle was passing him.

Carlos faked the handoff and lowered the ball beside his left leg. The defense couldn't see it there.

Kyle ran right, pretending that he had the ball, and drew two Huskies linebackers off the play. Meanwhile, the safeties up field were sticking tight to Andrew, just like Carlos thought they would be.

The Huskies' whole defense was busy covering Kyle and Andrew.

Carlos was open to run. He cut up the left side of the field. The Huskies linebackers finally caught on to what was happening and tore after him.

Meanwhile, the play clock reached zero. If Carlos didn't make it, the Wildcats would lose to the Huskies yet again!

But Carlos was too quick, and the linebackers were too far away. Carlos made it into the end zone before any Huskies could even touch him.

Carlos held the football up and cheered. The rest of the offense ran over and knocked him down in celebration. Everyone was happy and excited.

"Great play, Carlos," Coach French said. "You called a bootleg, saw your options, and made the best choice."

Andrew nodded. "I couldn't shake those safeties," he said. "Great call, Carlos. We finally beat the Huskies."

Carlos pulled off his helmet. "Thanks," he said. "I guess I'm not interested in being a superstar quarterback. I'm just happy to be a good quarterback."

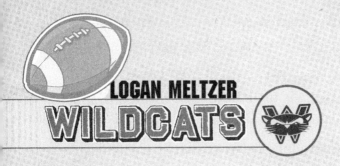

LOGAN MELTZER

WILDCATS

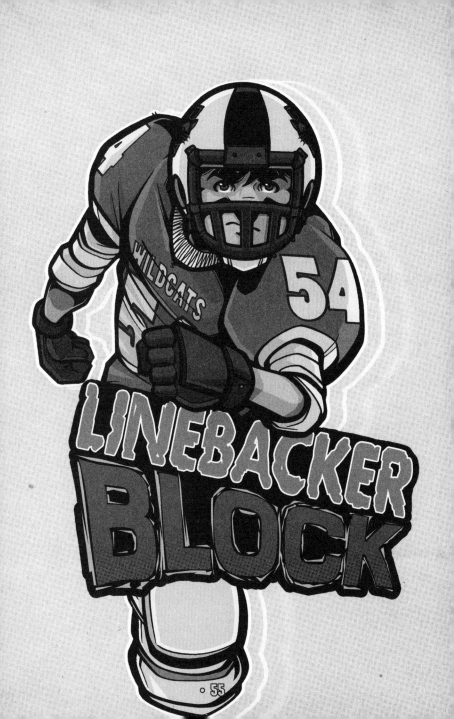

TABLE OF CONTENTS

The sun was going down on a Saturday evening in Westfield. Most of the eighth graders were out with their friends, down at Taco Paco's, at the movie theater on the north side of town, or maybe just hanging out at someone's house, playing video games.

But Logan Meltzer was all by himself. He was sitting in the TV room in the basement of his house.

He had the remote control in his right hand and was flipping through all one hundred and fifty-eight channels at blinding speed.

A news show. A boring music video. Cartoons. Something in Japanese. A lady cooking fish. A man in a boat, fishing. Nothing was on.

Logan heard someone coming. The *thud-thud-thud* of someone on the steps got louder and louder. Logan knew it had to be his dad.

"Logan!" his dad's voice called. The door to the TV room opened.

Logan's father was a very big man. In fact, Logan took after his dad, which was one of the reasons Logan was a good linebacker. He wasn't as tall as his dad, but he was strong.

Logan's dad was over six feet tall, and weighed about three hundred pounds. When he walked into the room, he huffed from his nose. Logan always thought it made him look like a bull.

"What are you doing down here all alone?" his dad asked.

Logan glanced at his father, then back at the TV. "I'm watching TV," he said.

His dad sighed and then dropped down on the couch next to Logan.

"I'm worried about you, Logan," his dad said. "Back in River City, you would never be home alone, flipping through the channels — not on a Saturday night!"

Logan kept pushing buttons on the remote, barely stopping for an instant to see what was what. "That's easy for you to say," Logan said. "You and Mom are going out tonight with your friends from River City. I can't, because I can't drive back to River City whenever I feel like it."

Logan's dad nodded. "I know," he said. "It doesn't seem fair."

"Yeah. Because it isn't fair," Logan said.

His dad groaned and rubbed his neck. "Logan, we've been over this," he said. "It will get easier. What about the guys on the football team?"

Logan shrugged and looked at his dad. "What about the guys on the team?" he repeated.

"Don't those guys go out on a Saturday night?" his dad said. "Maybe to a movie, or to the skating rink, or something?"

"The skating rink?" Logan said with a laugh. "Dad, come on."

"I don't know!" his dad replied, shrugging. "When I was young, we went roller-skating. What do I know?"

"Not much," Logan said, smiling. "Well, I guess I can be glad I don't have to play against my old team. We're not playing River City this season. I checked the schedule."

"Good, good," his dad said. "And listen. This will get easier for you, Logan. You'll get to know the kids in school and on the team. You won't be stuck at home on Saturdays for much longer."

Logan nodded. "I know," he said. "Hey, I'm going to send an email to Scotty Hansen back home." He got up from the couch and clicked the TV off. "I mean," he added quickly, "back in River City."

His dad laughed and headed up the steps.

CHAPTER 2

After school on Monday, Logan plodded down
the hall toward the locker room. The football
team had practice every day after school. Logan
pushed through the locker room door and sat on
the bench in front of his locker.

At least I have the football team, Logan thought
as he pulled open his locker. He put on his pads
for practice and found his practice jersey in the
back of his locker.

He picked it up and gave it a sniff. He
wrinkled up his nose at the stench. "Oops," he
said aloud.

Someone laughed as Logan turned around. It was Andrew, a wide receiver. "Forgot to bring that home to wash it, huh?" Andrew asked.

"Yeah, I guess," Logan said. He didn't know if Andrew was making fun of him or just being friendly. It was hard to tell. Andrew laughed again and then walked off toward his own locker.

Logan wrinkled his nose as he put on his smelly jersey. Then he grabbed his helmet and headed out to the field. Most of the team was already gathered on the sidelines, on or around the bench. The coach, Greg French, stood in front of the guys on the team.

Coach was in his blue and white Wildcats jacket, and he was wearing his blue and white Wildcats hat, like always. He also always had a whistle around his neck, and he was usually holding a clipboard.

"Okay, everyone," the coach said. Logan found an empty spot at the end of the bench and sat down.

Everyone was talking, and no one paid attention to the coach.

Luckily, Coach French was a nice guy, who always let the players have a few minutes to hang out before practice started.

"Let's quiet down, okay?" Coach French went on. "I need to announce some changes to the schedule for the week."

The team got quiet.

"So, this Friday's game," the coach said, "has been changed. It seems that some teams were playing each other too often, or not often enough. I don't know what happened."

He looked down at his clipboard and flipped through the papers. "The point is," he said, looking up at the team, "this Friday we'll be playing River City, not Wheaton."

Logan's eyes shot open. He thought he might throw up.

The coach looked right at him. "That's where you moved from, Logan. Isn't that right?" Coach French asked.

Logan swallowed and nodded. "Right, Coach," he said. "I played on the River City team last year, in seventh grade."

All of the other players turned and looked at him.

"So, can we count on you to tell us all their secret plays?" the coach asked. He looked at Logan with a hard stare.

Logan stared at him. All of a sudden, he wondered if Coach French wasn't as nice as he'd thought. "Um, well . . ." he mumbled.

Suddenly the coach burst out laughing. "I'm just kidding, Logan," he said, smiling. "Don't worry!" The rest of the team started laughing too, and Logan tried to smile. But inside, he felt terrible.

It seemed like his new team was making fun of him. To make matters worse, in a few days, he'd have to play football against his old teammates — his best friends!

CHAPTER 3

MEATLOAF

Logan walked really slowly on the way home from school that day. His body was sore from practice, but mainly he was feeling down.

He didn't have the energy to move fast. Even though his family's house wasn't far from the school, it took him almost an hour to get home from practice.

"Logan!" his mother called when he walked in. "You're so late!"

She came out of the kitchen. She was still in her suit from work, but she was also wearing oven mitts on both hands.

"Dinner's ready," she said.

Logan's mom was a tiny woman, not more than five feet tall, and she looked like a strong breeze would knock her over. When she and Logan's dad hugged or danced, Logan always thought she might get crushed.

"Sorry I'm late, Mom," Logan said. He followed her back into the kitchen. His dad was waiting at the table. "Hi, Dad. Sorry I'm late," said Logan.

His dad shrugged his big shoulders. "You're just in time for supper," he said, "so no harm done."

Logan sat down and watched as his mom put a meatloaf on the table. The meatloaf wasn't homemade. It was in an aluminum foil pan.

"Frozen meatloaf, huh?" Logan asked.

His dad chuckled and started slicing the meatloaf. "It's great," he said. "I lived on this frozen meatloaf in college."

The meatloaf turned out to be not too bad. Soon, Logan was stuffed full. "That was good, Mom," he said. "Thanks."

Hey, Logan!

What's up? Not much is
were still around to har

So you probably heard b
Cyclones are playing you
They changed the schedu

How cool is that? I though
going to get a chance to p
together this year, but it lo
after all.

I'm pretty excited. See you
afternoon!

Scotty

"Any plans tonight?" Dad asked as Logan cleared the table.

Logan shook his head. "Nope. I'm just going to do my homework and hang out here, I guess," he said. Then he headed downstairs.

He thought about turning on the TV, but decided to wait until he was done with his homework.

He sat down at the desk and turned on his computer. He was hoping he'd have an email back from his friend Scotty, and sure enough, he did.

Hey, Logan!

What's up? Not much is new here. Wish you were still around to hang out with.

So you probably heard by now that the Cyclones are playing your team on Friday. They changed the schedule!

How cool is that? I thought we weren't going to get a chance to play any ball together this year, but it looks like we will after all.

I'm pretty excited. See you on Friday afternoon!
Scotty

Logan clicked "reply," but then just stared at the blank email. What could he say? He wasn't excited about the game at all. In fact, it was tearing him apart.

So, instead of typing anything, he just closed the blank email and flicked off the monitor. Then he dropped onto the couch and started flipping through the TV channels again.

CHAPTER 4

At lunch on Friday, Logan was waiting in line in the cafeteria. It was pizza day. Logan tapped his fingers on his tray as he waited.

"Hey, Logan," someone said behind him. Logan turned. It was Andrew, the wide receiver from the football team.

"Oh, hi, Andrew," Logan said.

Andrew smacked his lips. "Man, I love pizza day," he said. He peeked around Logan to get a look at the line.

"What's taking so long up there?" Andrew called out. "I want my lunch!"

The woman behind the counter waved at him. "You keep it down, Andrew," she said, smiling. "You'll get your lunch."

Andrew laughed and then looked at Logan. "So we're playing your old team in a few hours, huh?" he asked.

Logan nodded. "Yeah," he said. The line inched up slowly. "Is that going to be weird?" Andrew asked. "I mean, I can't imagine having to play against the guys on the Wildcats. And all I have to do is run and catch."

"What do you mean? Why would it be weird?" Logan asked. "Playing is playing."

They had reached the food. Logan got two square pieces of pizza. He also took a bowl of vanilla pudding and a bowl of peas and carrots.

Andrew turned to the server and smiled. "I want four slices, Carol," he said. "Let me have four slices. Please!"

Carol, the server, laughed. "Hey, Andrew," she said, "if you're paying for two lunches, you're getting two lunches." She gave him the four slices he'd asked for and laughed again.

"Why would it be weird to play against my old team?" Logan asked again after they paid.

"Well," Andrew said as they left the line and headed toward the tables, "you'll be rushing their quarterback, going after their running backs . . . you know, tackling them. I don't know, I think that would be pretty tough."

Andrew shook his head and headed to the table at the far side of the room, where the whole football team was having lunch.

When Logan didn't follow him, Andrew turned around. "Hey, man," he said. "Why don't you come over and eat lunch with the rest of the team today? Just because you're the new guy doesn't mean you have to eat lunch alone."

Logan looked down at his pizza. He thought about what Andrew had said.

Logan was going to have to play against his old friends. He'd have to do his best to make sure the River City quarterback couldn't complete a single pass.

Even worse, Scotty was a running back. He'd have to tackle Scotty.

Logan looked back at Andrew, who was standing there waiting for him.

"Actually, um," Logan said, "I'm supposed to be meeting with Mr. Goulet, um, about my French class project. So I better head to his office."

That was a lie. Logan just couldn't bring himself to have lunch with his new football team. It felt like he was cheating on a friend.

Andrew squinted at Logan. "Okay," he said. "Sounds like fun."

Logan shrugged. "Yeah," he said, heading to the door. "I don't have a choice though, I guess."

He quickly left the cafeteria, carrying his tray of lunch. He headed for the library, where he hid in a corner to eat his pizza. It felt like rocks in his stomach.

CHAPTER 5

THE FIRST HALF

That afternoon, Logan sat on the Wildcats bench. The special team took the field to receive the first kickoff.

It was still weird for Logan to watch his own team come onto the field in blue and white. He wasn't used to the uniform or the team name. When the Cyclones took the field, he felt his spirits rise watching the players, with their familiar maroon jerseys and the silver tornado logo on their helmets.

Logan watched the start of the game from the bench.

He was very glad his team had the ball first, not because it was an advantage, but because it meant he wouldn't have to take the field for a little while.

The Cyclones defense wasn't bad, he decided, although he was almost sorry to admit it. *They don't seem to be missing me*, he thought as he watched.

On third down, a huge hole opened in the Wildcats offensive line. *I could have gotten through there if I were still on the Cyclones*, he thought.

But his old teammates missed the chance. The Wildcats connected a twenty-yard pass and got a first down.

On the bench, the other defensive players cheered. Logan didn't even think about cheering. For a moment, he had forgotten which team he was on.

When Logan didn't get up, the others looked at him, and he felt stupid. Logan decided to make up for it. He clapped his hands and shouted, "Good job, offense! Keep it up!" But then he felt even stupider for being so late with his cheer.

Logan frowned. *Whatever*, he thought. *We shouldn't have completed that pass anyway, with that weak blocking.*

The Wildcats scored a touchdown on the drive and got the extra point. When Logan took the field after the kickoff, his team was winning 7-0.

* * *

Logan stood behind the defensive line. As a linebacker, he started standing, while the linemen started bent over with one hand on the grass. That way, Logan could see over the line and call out to the other players what the offense might be planning.

On first down, Logan spotted some motion. He called out to his teammates to watch for the run to the left side.

Then he spotted the Cyclones running back's number and name on his jersey.

It was his friend Scotty Hansen.

"Hut, hut!" the Cyclones quarterback shouted. "Hike!" And he took the snap.

Right away, he turned to his right and handed off to Scotty.

Scotty shot toward the left side and then cut up the field.

Logan moved in to close off the hole in his defensive line, but Scotty spun and got around him. Logan ended up on the grass. He watched Scotty make a ten-yard run. One of the other Wildcat linebackers finally got him down at the forty.

Logan got to his feet. Suddenly Scotty was next to him. He was smiling and out of breath.

"Hey, Logan," Scotty said. "Are you out of shape or something?"

Logan looked at him. "What do you mean?" he asked.

"I could never get past you in scrimmages last year," Scotty said. "Either you're out of shape, or I've gotten much better."

Logan tried to laugh as Scotty patted him on the pads and walked to the River City huddle. But then Logan turned and saw one of the other defensive players from the Wildcats.

"Hey, James," Logan said. But James only glared at him, then walked off.

Great, Logan thought. *He probably thinks I let Scotty get by because he's my friend.*

But then Logan wondered if he really had tried as hard as he could. The truth was, he didn't know.

CHAPTER 6

NICE PASS

The Cyclones' drive up the field continued to go well. Logan tried hard to stop their forward motion. But he felt torn.

Why did this game have to be against River City? he asked himself. *Why couldn't we play against a different team, a team that wasn't made up of my best friends? Trying to beat strangers would be easier.*

The Cyclones were lined up at the Wildcats' thirty-yard line. It was third down. On this play, if the defense could stop them, the Cyclones would have their last chance for six points. It was up to the defense to keep them to three points at most.

"Hut!" the Cyclones quarterback shouted. "Hike!"

The Cyclones center snapped the ball. Logan watched the quarterback pull back. He faked the handoff to Scotty, who went out wide to the right. Logan saw the screen pass just before it happened. He sprinted through a hole in the line as the pass left the quarterback's hand.

Then Logan felt worried. *I can't intercept a pass to Scotty*, he thought. *He's my best friend!*

Logan slowed down. He didn't really mean to. It just happened. At the last second, he leaped for the ball, hoping everyone would see how hard he was trying. But it was too late. The perfect pass sailed over his fingertips and Scotty caught it.

Logan sprawled out on the grass and lifted his head. He was just able to get to his feet in time to watch his old friend — and new rival — run into the end zone for six points.

River City would tie it up with the extra point. Logan knew he could have stopped them. But did he want to?

CHAPTER 7

BAD DAY

Logan jogged over to the bench. Andrew was putting on his helmet, getting ready for the offense's turn on the field. "Hey, Logan," he said. "You seem pretty slow out there today."

Logan swallowed. "I do?" he asked. But he knew it was true.

"Yeah," Andrew replied. "Are you feeling all right?" He didn't wait for an answer. "Maybe Otis can come in for you. "I'm sure he'd like the chance to play. We can talk to the coach if you need a rest." Andrew patted Logan's shoulder pads.

"No, I'm fine," Logan said.

Andrew shrugged and headed out to the field, while Logan dropped onto the bench, feeling miserable.

The Wildcats' offense had another good drive. Andrew made an excellent catch on second down and took the ball all the way to the Cyclones' forty-yard line.

Everyone on the bench went crazy. Even Logan got up and cheered.

Everyone sure is playing hard, he thought. He wished it were as easy for him to pick a side.

On the next few plays, the Cyclones' defense was very strong, and the Wildcats were forced to kick the field goal. That gave them the lead going into halftime. But with the score at 10-7, the Wildcats were only up by three points.

If Logan and the defense couldn't stop the Cyclones, River City would easily tie it up. They could even take the lead.

The feeling in the locker room at halftime didn't match the feeling in Logan's stomach.

Everyone was in a great mood. After all, they were up by three points. A few players on the offense were having a really good game so far. Everyone was pretty sure that they'd win the game.

But even though he was cheering along with the rest of the team as they took their halftime break, Logan felt sick. A small part of his brain kept thinking, *If it weren't for me, we'd be up by ten points!*

CHAPTER 8

HALFTIME

"Everyone settle down, all right?" the coach said. The players all took a seat on a bench or leaned against the lockers or walls.

Logan stood toward the back of the group and looked at his feet. He watched the other members of the team high-five each other as they started to quiet down. Finally Coach French blew his whistle and the room fell silent.

"I'm glad you're all excited," the coach said with a smile, "but as far as I can tell, we still have half this game to go."

A few players mumbled in reply.

"And we're only up by three points," the coach added. "So don't get too confident, and don't think we have this game in the bag, okay?"

"Okay, Coach," the team replied all together.

"All right," Coach French said. He nodded. "Now then, let's go over a few things. . . ."

Logan didn't pay very close attention as the coach rattled off some plays that hadn't worked well and mentioned some defensive mistakes. He felt like he didn't need to hear about those. After all, those mistakes had been his fault!

When the coach was done with his speech, he found Logan.

"Logan, I noticed you seem a little sluggish out there," Coach French said. "I've seen you block tougher passes in practice than that screen on the Cyclones' first drive."

"I really went for it, Coach," Logan said. "I just missed it. The pass went right past my fingertips."

The coach looked at him. "Okay, Logan," he said. "As long as you're giving it your all out there."

He patted Logan on the shoulder and walked off, looking down at his clipboard.

Then Logan saw that Andrew had been standing behind the coach. He had overheard the conversation.

"I guess Coach noticed the same thing I did, huh?" Andrew asked.

"Man!" Logan said. "I wish you'd stop giving me such a hard time. So I'm having a bad day, and my jersey stinks because I forgot to wash it, and I eat lunch alone! So what?"

Andrew took a step back and smiled. "Whoa, whoa," he said, putting his hands up. "Take it easy. I didn't mean to make you angry. Calm down."

Logan took a deep breath. "Sorry," he said. "I guess I'm having kind of a rough game."

"So what's the problem?" Andrew asked.

"Isn't it obvious?" Logan said. "The guys on the Cyclones — some of them are my best friends. Their running back, Scotty Hansen, used to come over to my house after school almost every day, because his mom worked late."

Logan sighed. Then he went on, "We went to school together for eight years. We grew up together. And we've played ball together since we were like, five. How am I supposed to play against him?"

"Oh, I hear you," Andrew replied. "I don't think I'd like having to play football against the guys on the Wildcats. That would be really hard. They're my best friends."

"Exactly," Logan said, shaking his head.

Andrew glanced up at the game clock. The second half was about to start.

"We should get out there," Andrew said. "But you know what?"

"What?" Logan asked.

"I think maybe it isn't about being a bad friend," Andrew said. "Because really all of us are just out here because we love playing football, right?"

"Right," Logan replied. "I guess that's why I've always played. Scotty too. He loves the game as much as I do."

"So the truth is, if you're not trying to stop Hansen from running the ball or catching that screen pass," Andrew went on, "then Hansen doesn't get to play real football."

Andrew pushed open the doors to the field. "He might as well go play with the peewee league," he added. "Know what I mean?"

Logan nodded as he walked through the door. "Yeah," he said. "I know exactly what you mean."

CHAPTER 9

SECOND HALF

The second half started with the Wildcats kicking off to the Cyclones. That meant Logan was on the field in his two-point stance almost right away.

Logan stood tall over the line. He spotted Scotty in motion. "Watch for the handoff," Logan shouted to his teammates.

"Hike!" called the Cyclones quarterback.

Scotty came running up behind him and went for the handoff. But the quarterback faked and drew back from the pocket.

"He's passing!" Logan called out.

He spotted Scotty running fast toward the left sideline, and he ran after him.

"Screen left!" Logan shouted to his line. Two of the other linemen pulled back from rushing the quarterback and chased Scotty just as the pass was released.

But Logan was even quicker. He wasn't close enough to intercept, but he launched through the air and got one finger on the ball. It was enough to send it tumbling to the grass.

"Nice block, Logan!" another linemen called out. He felt a few hands pat his helmet and smiled.

"Nice one, Logan," a familiar voice said. It was Scotty. He was smiling, too. "Glad to see you came out to play today. Finally."

Scotty jogged back to his own team's huddle. Logan lined up with the defenders.

That's right, he thought. *I am here to play. It's about time.*

"All right, D," he shouted to his teammates, clapping his hands. "Let's keep 'em stopped right here."

The other defensive players hooted and clapped with him. And Logan finally felt like he was on the right team.

CHAPTER 10

NEW FRIENDS

Logan's defensive line was really giving it their all for the whole second half. When the referee blew the whistle for the two-minute warning, the Wildcats were up by ten points.

Logan watched his team march up the field from the bench. He clapped and hollered along with everyone else after every complete pass and every run.

Coach French walked over and patted Logan's helmet. "You've really improved in this second half," the coach said. "Maybe good enough for today's MVP award. You must be warmed up."

"Sort of," Logan replied. "It was something Andrew said to me before the second half started. Kind of gave me my energy back."

"Well, remind me to make him MVP, then," the coach said with a laugh. "Keep up the good work out there. You're doing great."

* * *

In the end, the Wildcats won 24-7. And just like he'd said he would, after the game, Coach French named Logan the MVP of the game.

Logan finished showering and changing and was heading out of the locker room when Andrew walked up to him. The Wildcats quarterback, Carlos, was there too.

"You guys, we should go out and celebrate," Andrew said. "Let's go down to Paco's and get some tacos and then catch a movie or something."

"Definitely!" Carlos said. "Logan, I can't remember the last time someone on the defensive squad got MVP."

Logan smiled. "That sounds good," he said as the three boys reached the parking lot. Then he spotted someone across the pavement.

"Hey, Scotty!" Logan called out.

His old friend from River City waved. Logan called him over.

"Why don't you join us for some tacos," Logan said. "And then maybe we can catch that new horror movie."

Scotty looked from Logan to Carlos and to Andrew. "Um, sure," Scotty said. "Okay."

Andrew laughed. "Man, don't worry," he said. "We're all just playing football. It doesn't mean we have to hate each other."

Logan nodded. "That's right," he said. "That's why, even though I don't hate you and the other guys on the Cyclones, we still beat you guys."

Carlos and Andrew cracked up laughing. Scotty smiled. "Ha ha," he said. "You're just lucky you won't have to face us again this season."

The three Wildcats laughed at that too.

Logan looked around.

On one side, he had an old friend from River City. On the other side, he had two new friends, from the Wildcats.

We all love football, he thought. *And I'm starting to love my school.*

As the sun went down behind the water tower, the four friends headed down the road to Taco Paco's.

TABLE OF CONTENTS

CHAPTER 1

ALL - STAR

The roar of the crowd was deafening. They screamed and cheered, "Andrew! Andrew! Andrew!"

Andrew Tucker smiled through the cage of his helmet. He had scored the winning touchdown of his most important game ever. The fans snapped photos as he danced in the end zone. They all knew someday he'd be the most famous wide receiver in the country.

Scouts from every college and half of the pro teams in the country were watching too. They took notes and shot video footage.

Someone tapped Andrew on the shoulder and he turned. The sun was behind his dad's head, and Andrew squinted.

"Are you listening to me, Andrew?" his dad said.

"Huh?" Andrew replied.

Dad laughed. "I think that you've been daydreaming again," he said. "What are you thinking about this time?"

Andrew sighed. "Same as ever," he said.

The truth was, Andrew wasn't an all-star wide receiver. He played for the junior high football team, and he even got to start most games. But he was lucky if he made one reception per game and one touchdown per season.

The real all-star was Andrew's brother, Marcus. Andrew and his dad were at the Westfield High School Wildcats game right now, and Andrew was dreaming that he was as great as his brother.

Marcus was the one with college and pro scouts watching him. Marcus was the one with adoring fans.

Marcus was the one who had just scored the game-winning touchdown . . . again. It was Marcus's tenth touchdown of the season, and it was only the third game.

Dad stood up from the bleacher. "Another great game for the Wildcats," he said. "I'll get the car. You get your brother."

When Dad had walked off, Andrew got up and headed toward the Wildcats bench. It was crowded with people celebrating and shaking Marcus's hand.

Marcus had fans of all ages. There were other high school guys, some high school girls, plenty of team parents, and even some very old men. Andrew knew that some of those men had played on the Westfield Wildcats when they were teenagers, fifty or sixty years ago.

"Hey, Marcus," Andrew called out. "Come on, bro." He got up on his toes to see over the crowd surrounding his brother. "We have to go."

Marcus shook a few more hands and even signed some little kid's jersey. "Okay, little bro," he said. "Give me a minute."

Andrew stepped back from the crowd and sat on the bench. After a few more minutes, the people went away.

The two brothers walked toward Dad's car. Marcus put an arm around his brother's shoulder. "What's wrong?" he asked.

Andrew didn't know what to say. He couldn't admit he was jealous of his brother or that he wanted to be as great on the field as Marcus was.

Just then, Dad honked the horn. The two brothers rounded the school and spotted the car.

"Race ya!" Marcus said. Even though he had his shoulder pads under one arm and his helmet in one hand, he took off like a shot.

Andrew didn't even try to keep up. "That's why I'm down," he muttered, even though Marcus couldn't hear him. "You're fast, like a wide receiver should be. And I'm not."

CHAPTER 2

RUNNING PLAYS

The Westfield Middle School Wildcats practiced every day after school. Andrew usually looked forward to practice, but on Monday afternoon, he was still feeling down.

"Look alive out there, Andrew," Coach French called out.

"Sorry, Coach," Andrew yelled back.

He sighed. He couldn't get himself motivated. After a few laps on the track, the team had been running the same old plays over and over. Only one was a long passing play, so Andrew was pretty bored.

The quarterback, Carlos Suarez, counted off. "Hut, hut," he shouted. "Two, two, hut!"

The snap was good. Carlos drew back into the pocket.

Andrew went up the right line and then cut across. But play two wasn't a passing play. Andrew's job would be to fake out one defender and then block for the running.

Sure enough, Carlos handed off the ball to Noah Frank, a second-string running back. Then, since this was only a drill, the coach blew the whistle to stop the play.

Andrew took a deep breath and headed back to the line.

"Nice job, guys," the coach said. "Andrew, I want to see a little more speed out there. Carlos might decide to look for you if the defensive line is too strong."

"Can we work on my speed, Coach?" Andrew replied. "Do some running drills, maybe?"

Coach French shook his head. "Right now, we need to get these plays down so we can run them cleanly in next week's game."

"How am I going to improve my speed if we only ever practice plays?" Andrew asked.

"I mean, it's just drills," he went on, "so everyone is moving in slow motion, practically. Did you see Noah take that handoff? I think my great-grandma could move faster, and she's ninety-eight!"

A few guys laughed, but Noah looked at his feet. He wasn't the best running back on the team, but he loved the game. Andrew felt bad right away.

"That's enough from you, Andrew," Coach French said, frowning. "One more comment like that, and your speed won't matter. You'll be benched for the rest of the season. Are we clear?"

"Yeah, yeah," Andrew said.

He kicked the dirt in front of him. *The field isn't even any good for football*, he thought. *Too dusty. Can't they even keep the grass alive at this school?*

The coach went on, "We do sprints every day, and we do warm-up laps and warm-down laps every practice. It's all we have time for."

He clapped once, then said, "Okay, guys. Enough distractions. Let's try that bootleg Carlos has been working on. Line up!"

The team clapped, then got into formation. Andrew was last in line.

CHAPTER 3

GET LEGS

"Look at that," Marcus said. He was leaning forward on the ratty basement couch, holding tight to the video game controller. His mouth was hanging open in a smile, and his eyes were glazed over. "Ooh, check this out."

Andrew leaned back in the corner of the couch. He watched the TV screen as Marcus tried to beat the last team in their new video game, Soccer Championship.

"Goal!" Marcus shouted. He dropped the controller and jumped off the couch. Then he spun to face Andrew. "Who is the champion?"

"Man, sit down," Andrew said. "It's just a video game."

"Ha," Marcus said. "You're just jealous of all my skills." But he dropped back down to the couch.

"Yeah, I am jealous," Andrew admitted, "but not of that dumb soccer game. I'm jealous because I'm too slow on the football field."

"What?" Marcus asked. "Who told you you were slow?"

"No one has to tell me," Andrew said. "I know it because I see you out there, like a bolt of lightning. I can't do that."

"Does Coach French work on speed with you?" Marcus asked.

"Not really," Andrew replied. "We spend most of the time going over plays, until everyone has them memorized."

Marcus nodded. He said, "The coach's top priority is to build a winning team. He can't focus all his time and energy on just one player. He's not trying to make stars. Just football players."

Andrew sighed.

"Don't feel bad," Marcus added. He slapped his brother on the knee. "Remember, it's you that needs to make sure you're the best receiver you can be. It's true for you, and for me, and for every great receiver ever, at every level of the game."

Andrew shook his head. "At least the high school coach helps you with speed drills," he said.

"Yeah," Marcus said, shrugging. "I got some help along the way, no doubt. But it's my legs that take me down the field like a rocket, you know?" He got up and struck a pose like the Heisman Trophy, and then laughed.

"I don't have your legs," Andrew said. "I have mine."

"That's not what I mean," Marcus said. "It's not just about legs, man."

"So what do you mean?" Andrew asked.

But Marcus just shook his head. "Let's get upstairs," he said, then sniffed the air. "I think dinner's ready."

CHAPTER 4

GETTING IT

The next morning, Andrew sat at the table eating cereal. He took a sip of orange juice.

"Hey, little brother," Marcus said, walking in. Andrew smiled, then ate a bite of cereal.

"So," Marcus said, "have you thought about what I said yesterday, before supper?" He grabbed his running shoes from the closet and slipped them on.

"I guess," Andrew said. "But it didn't make any sense. Your legs take you down the field. Duh. And mine take me down the field too, only way more slowly."

Marcus got down on one knee to tie his sneaker. "That's true," he said. Then he switched knees to tie the other sneaker.

"What does that have to do with Coach French?" Andrew asked. He pushed his bowl of cereal away from him and finished the juice. "He still won't let us run speed drills, so I won't be getting any faster."

"Nope," Marcus said, "not just by going to practice. You're probably right."

"So what's your advice?" Andrew asked.

"Look at it this way," Marcus said. He pulled open the door and looked back at his brother. "How are you getting to school today?"

Andrew shrugged. "The bus," he said. "Why?"

Marcus smirked and raised his eyebrows. Then he slipped on his earphones and jogged out the door and down the sidewalk.

Andrew smiled. *I get it*, he thought.

CHAPTER 5

LONG PRACTICE

At practice that afternoon, the team ran two laps together and did some wind sprints. After that, Andrew mostly ran up the field. Carlos threw passes to him exactly twice.

"I don't know why I bother washing my jersey," Andrew said after practice. He was walking back to the locker room with Logan, a linebacker. "I never even break a sweat."

Logan chuckled. "At least we have all the plays down, right?" he said. "The defensive line is really playing great. And the offense looked pretty good today too."

In the locker room, Andrew peeled off his pads and his jersey, but he left on his football pants and sneakers. He shut his locker with a bang.

"Um, Andrew?" Logan said. He was tying his sneakers, dressed in jeans and a nice shirt. "Forgetting something?"

"What do you mean?" Andrew asked.

"I mean you're still wearing half your uniform," Logan said. "Are you going to ride the bus like that?"

Andrew shook his head. "I'm not going to ride the bus at all," he said. "For me, practice isn't over yet." He saluted Logan and headed outside.

The air was already cooling off after the warm fall day. The sun was setting behind Andrew as he jogged quickly along South Street toward his neighborhood.

"I can do this," he said to himself between breaths. "If this is what it takes to be great, then I'm up for the challenge."

At the corner of Ninth Street, he jogged in place for a minute. His backpack bounced on his shoulders. When the light changed, he ran on.

Soon, he spotted his house at the end of a long block and started sprinting.

When Andrew stepped through the front door, he checked the clock. 6:45.

"Not too bad," he said, short of breath.

His dad stepped out of the kitchen. "'Not too bad?'" he asked angrily. "Where have you been?"

Andrew tried to catch his breath. "I jogged," he said. "I jogged home. I thought it —"

"You are home an hour later than normal, Andrew!" his dad said, interrupting him. "When I agreed to let you join the football team, you promised to be home for dinner every night and to do your homework the minute you got home."

"I know, Dad, but —" Andrew started, but his dad cut him off again.

"Now you've missed dinner, and your homework still isn't done," Dad said.

Andrew kneeled down to take off his sneakers. "I'm sorry," he said quietly.

Dad nodded. "Okay. Now get changed and washed up," he said. "Then eat your dinner. It's cold."

With that, Dad stepped back into the kitchen. Andrew heard his father's chair scrape the floor as Dad sat down to finish his supper.

Andrew put his football sneakers in the front closet and peeked into the kitchen. Dad had his back to him. Marcus was quietly enjoying his spaghetti. He looked up and saw Andrew.

Andrew glared at him. Then he mouthed, "Thanks a lot."

Marcus shrugged. "Not my fault," he mouthed back.

Andrew shook his head and went upstairs to clean up.

CHAPTER 6

LATE TO BED

By the time Andrew got done showering, eating, and doing all his homework, it was late. With a big yawn, he pushed back his chair and stretched his arms and back.

There was a knock at the door. "Come in," Andrew said.

His dad opened the door. "Is your homework done?" he asked. He had calmed down a lot since dinner.

"Yeah," Andrew said. "Just finished. I didn't realize how tough that math assignment was going to be. I think I went through ten pencils."

Dad laughed and sat down on the bed. "I'm sorry for getting so angry," Dad said. "But first of all, you need to let me know when you'll be late for supper."

"I know," Andrew said. "I should have called."

Dad nodded. "Second, if your homework is tough, we need to work on it," he said. "And that means you come straight home after practice so we can do that."

Andrew picked at the corner of his math textbook. He didn't look at his dad, just stared down at the book.

"What are you not saying, son?" Dad asked.

Andrew pushed the book away and faced his father.

"I need to work on my speed, Dad," Andrew said. "Marcus jogged to and from school every day. He worked hard to get fast so he could be a great receiver. I want to do the same thing."

Dad smiled. "I'm glad you look up to your brother," he said. "He's a hard worker and a great athlete. And I'm glad that you want to do the hard work to be great at football."

Andrew glanced at the wall. It was covered with posters of great receivers: Jerry Rice, Randy Moss, Steve Largent.

"But you're young, Andrew," Dad went on. "You need to focus on academics, not athletics. If you can do both, like your brother, that's great. But if it comes down to a conflict between the two, you already know what I'm going to decide."

Dad got up and headed to the door. He glanced at his watch.

"Now, it's late," he said. "You need to get some sleep."

"Especially if I plan to get up early to jog to school tomorrow," Andrew said.

Dad laughed. "That's right," he said. "Good night."

Andrew leaned back in his chair after his dad left the room. He knew he couldn't change his dad's mind. If Andrew wanted to have time to practice and get his speed up, he'd have to find a way to get every bit of homework done too.

 EARLY TO RISE

When Andrew's father stepped into the kitchen the next morning, Andrew was tying his sneakers. "What are you doing up?" Dad asked. "It's not even seven."

Andrew glanced up at the hall clock. "Wow," he said. "I'm doing pretty well. See you later."

"Wait a minute!" Dad said as Andrew opened the front door. "Why are you leaving so early?"

"I'm going to jog to school," Andrew said. "There's no way this run will get in the way of my schoolwork, since normally I'd still be sleeping."

Dad scratched his beard and yawned. "I'd like

to be sleeping myself," he said. "But at least have some breakfast. You can't run hungry."

"I already ate," Andrew said, stepping outside. "Bye, Dad!" And with that, he took off running.

* * *

At lunch that day, Andrew stared at the pile of ravioli on his plate.

"Hey, Andrew," Logan said from the across the table. He glanced at Carlos and laughed. "Andrew."

Andrew's eyes felt heavy. He was hungry, but he couldn't bring himself to fork a ravioli and pop it into his mouth. Suddenly he felt an elbow in his ribs. "Hey!" he said. "What was that for?"

Carlos laughed. "Just wanted to make sure you were alive over there," he said.

"Really, Andrew," Logan added with a chuckle. "Were you up all night or something? You look like you're about to pass out."

"Oh, I got up extra early today," Andrew replied. "And I guess I went to bed pretty late last night, too. I jogged home after practice yesterday. And this morning I got up early to jog to school."

"Why?" Carlos asked.

Andrew shrugged. "If Coach French isn't going to give me time at practice to get my speed up, then I have to do it myself," he said. "That's what Marcus says."

Carlos shrugged. "Sounds okay to me," he said. "I wouldn't mind having a wide receiver as good as Marcus to throw to. I hope it works."

"Thanks," Andrew replied.

"Sure," Carlos said. "But I hope your new schedule isn't making you too tired. After all, today is game day."

Andrew dropped his plastic fork. "Oh no," he said. "I'm exhausted, and I forgot the game is this afternoon!"

CHAPTER 8

EXHAUSTED

Andrew's afternoon didn't go well. At one point during government class, Logan had to kick his foot to wake him up. The teacher nearly caught him sleeping.

"You're never going to make it through the whole game," Logan said as the two boys got changed into their uniforms after school. "Maybe you should tell the coach you're sick. You can go home and get some sleep."

Andrew stifled a yawn. "No way," he said. "I haven't been running and working on my speed just to go home and sleep."

Logan shrugged. "Okay," he said. "But I have a feeling you won't be moving too fast out there today."

Logan slammed his locker shut and headed out to the field. Andrew grabbed his helmet and sat on the bench.

"I have to get some energy," he said to himself. "I can't let one bad night's sleep ruin the game for me."

Andrew nodded to himself and closed his locker. "I can do this," he said. Then he headed out to the field.

As soon as he started running, Andrew knew he was more tired than he'd thought. His legs felt like rubber.

The game didn't start well. The first quarter was really tiring. During the second quarter, Carlos called a passing play. Andrew would have to sprint about fifteen yards off the line, then cut to the right.

"Hut, hut, hike!" Carlos called, and the center snapped the ball.

Carlos drew back, and Andrew took off from the line.

Carlos released the ball perfectly, but when Andrew cut to the right he lost his footing and slipped. The defender, who had kept up with Andrew easily, snatched the ball from the air.

"Interception!" Carlos called out.

The other team's player ran along the sideline for ten yards before being forced out of bounds.

"Look alive out there, Andrew!" Coach French called from the sidelines.

Andrew pulled off his helmet and headed to the bench with the rest of the offense. "Sorry, Coach," Andrew said. He dropped onto the bench.

Carlos stood in front of him. "So much for having a receiver as good as Marcus," Carlos said. "That was awful."

Andrew glared up at him. Carlos just shook his head and walked off.

At halftime, Andrew headed to the locker room. Marcus was waiting for him. Andrew's brother grabbed his arm. "Just a second, little brother," Marcus said. "I want to talk to you."

"What?" Andrew said. "I can't stand around out here. I'm not exactly popular on the team right now. If I miss the halftime huddle, I'll probably get expelled from school."

"I just need a minute," Marcus said. "You look pretty tired out there."

"Yeah," Andrew said. "I got up early."

"Dad told me," Marcus said. "He said you jogged to school today, too. Good for you."

Andrew shrugged.

"But you're making the same mistake I made at first," Marcus said. "It took me weeks to figure it out, so I'll let you in on my secret. Schedule."

"Schedule?" Andrew repeated.

"Simple, really," Marcus said. "But I failed a math test and got a D in Spanish before I figured it out. Dad was threatening to pull me off the football team."

"What did you do?" Andrew asked.

"I looked at my whole day," Marcus said. "I made choices. For example, I used to have lunch with some friends of mine. We'd take the whole half hour, goof off, start trouble in the cafeteria."

"Yeah," Andrew said, smiling. "That's what Logan and Carlos and I do."

"But I bet you get some homework in the morning, right?" Marcus asked.

"Sure," Andrew said. "I always do."

"You could have all that homework done by now if you worked while you ate, instead of goofing off," Marcus explained.

"I see what you mean," Andrew said.

Marcus patted him on the back. "Okay. Now get into that halftime meeting before they send you off to play for the other team," he said.

CHAPTER 9

TIMING

That night, after the game and after he'd done his homework, Andrew looked over his schedule. The next game was a week away. If he did his morning homework during lunch, he'd have extra time to run after school. If he skipped playing Championship Soccer with his brother some nights, he could get to bed early and be up in time for a morning run, too.

That week, Andrew was very busy. The morning after the game, he woke up early and ran sprints in the park near his house. He even had time to shower and catch the bus afterward.

At lunch, he spotted Logan and Carlos at their usual table, but he headed off to a quiet corner with his tray of food. Andrew pulled out his books and started his math homework. After a few minutes, he realized someone was standing behind him. He turned to look.

"Hi, Carlos," Andrew said. "Hi, Logan." His two teammates stood there, smiling at him.

"What are you doing?" Carlos said. "It's lunchtime. You're not supposed to be doing homework now."

"Yeah," Logan said. "What, did you leave your homework for the last minute? Is this due next period or something?"

Andrew shook his head. "Nope," he said. "This is the homework Ms. Finnegan assigned in math today. I'm getting it done now so I can work out tonight."

Carlos and Logan looked at each other. Then Carlos put a hand on Andrew's head. "Hm," he said. "He doesn't have a fever."

"Maybe we should call the nurse anyway," Logan said. "Just to be on the safe side."

"Ha ha," Andrew said without smiling. "You guys are hilarious. Now leave me alone so I can work."

Carlos shook his head. Logan slapped Andrew on the back as they walked away.

* * *

That weekend, Andrew had plenty of free time. Normally he'd spend it at the mall with his friends, or playing video games with his brother. Not this weekend, though. He had a game coming up, and he needed to get ready.

"Andrew!" his dad called. "Logan is on the phone. Are you meeting some guys from the team down at the mall today?"

Andrew was at the front door, putting on his sneakers. "No, Dad," he called back. "I'm going running. Tell Logan I'll see him Monday. We can hang out next weekend."

CHAPTER 10

WILDCATS vs. LIONS

As busy as he was, Andrew could hardly believe a week had gone by. But it was game day again, and this week, Westfield was facing their toughest rivals, the Lions from Libertyville Middle School.

This time, though, the game was going to be different. Andrew knew it. This time, he was ready. He wasn't tired. He was rested and in great shape.

In the first quarter, Andrew stepped up to Carlos before a huddle. "Throw it to me," he said. "I can lose this defender, easy."

Carlos shook his head. "And you can slip on the grass and give him the ball to catch, too, huh?" he said.

"That won't happen today," Andrew said. "Look, call whatever play you want. But keep an eye on me, okay?"

Carlos looked at Andrew. "Fine," he said. "I'll look for you, but no promises."

The boys joined the huddle. Carlos called an option, and then shouted, "Break!"

The offense formed their line and Carlos called for the snap: "Hut!"

Carlos drew back, and Andrew took off like a shot. He ran out about thirty yards, then cut hard back and to the left sideline. His defender cut too, but not as smoothly.

Andrew was wide open. Carlos was watching, and he drew back quickly and released for the long pass. It flew at Andrew's chest. Andrew closed his hands over the ball and dodged quickly as his defender dove at him.

Andrew turned toward the end zone, but two defenders were on top of him. He went down at the forty.

"Nice!" Carlos called out, clapping and running up to the new line of scrimmage.

Andrew jogged to the huddle. His teammates gave him high fives.

"Way to lose that defender, Andrew," Carlos said. "You're starting to look like Marcus out there."

Andrew smiled and got ready for the next play.

* * *

By the fourth quarter, the score was 7-10, Wildcats.

Andrew was playing his best, but passing games were tough. He'd made some nice receptions, but the Wildcats' points came from a quarterback sneak and one field goal.

Meanwhile, the Lions' short game was really on that day.

With only a few minutes left in the fourth quarter, their running back took a surprise hand-off. He ran up the sideline for forty yards and a touchdown.

After the extra point kick, the score was 14-10, Lions.

"All right, guys," Carlos said in the huddle after the kick-off. "We need to score, fast, if we're going to win this game."

"There's less than one minute left," one of the Wildcats linemen said. "This game is over. We have no chance."

"Nice attitude," Carlos replied, shaking his head. He looked at Andrew. "Can you lose that defender again?" Carlos asked.

"No problem," Andrew replied. "Just say when."

"Right now," Carlos said. "I want you to go as long as I can throw. Go out to their forty and cut to the right. I'll find you. Okay?"

Everyone nodded.

"Good," Carlos said. He clapped and said, "Break!"

At the line, Andrew's heart was racing. He thought about the last week and how hard he'd worked. He'd missed a couple of movies, and Marcus was now much better at Championship Soccer than he was.

But none of that mattered now. What mattered was the effort and the game.

"Hut," Carlos called. "Hut!"

The center snapped the ball, and Andrew took off running. He had five yards on his defender right away.

Andrew pumped his arms at his side. He was at the Lions' forty in no time, and he faked to the left, then turned right. He looked up just as Carlos released the pass.

Andrew's defender stumbled a bit when Andrew cut. By the time he recovered, the ball was at Andrew's open hands.

He caught the pass perfectly and took a sharp left toward the end zone. The field was wide open, from the forty to the one.

He was home free. And Andrew ran, as fast as he could.

Andrew's legs seemed to move on their own. He imagined he was on his own street, running over the broken sidewalk, past his neighbors' houses and the blue mailbox on the corner.

He smiled, and then kicked up his speed even more.

"Touchdown!" the referee called out, throwing up his arms.

Andrew stopped on the far side of the end zone and threw down the football. Then he pulled off his helmet and looked up at the clock. Only two seconds remained.

Carlos came sprinting up the field. "Now it's over," he shouted. The whole offense was right behind him. They picked Andrew up and carried him to the bench.

Coach French and Andrew's brother were there, cheering like crazy.

"Great reception, little brother," Marcus said, giving Andrew a high five. "I guess the schedule is working."

"You know it," Andrew said. "Thanks for all the help, bro."

Coach French said, "If you keep up this hard work, I have a feeling you'll be up against your brother in the pro draft before you know it."

Marcus and Andrew laughed.

"I don't know, Coach," Andrew said. "I think I'll keep making academics a priority for now."

The coach nodded. "Good idea," he said.

"Besides," Marcus added, "I'm sure Andrew and I will get a chance to face each other when we're both in the pros."

NOAH HART
WILDCATS

TABLE OF CONTENTS

CHAPTER 1

STATS GUY

While the Wildcats played against the Buccaneers in front of him, Noah Hart sat on the bench. His sports magazine was folded open on his left thigh. Under his helmet, on the bench next to him, was his big book of stats.

Noah's eyes stayed on the magazine. He scanned quickly through the article on a college running back. The writer thought a college player, Jack Tyler, was going to be a great NFL player. Lots of pro teams wanted to draft him as soon as he graduated, since he was so amazing.

Noah wasn't convinced.

"Look at this," he said to the player next to him, Adam Glick. "This article says Jack Tyler is going to be the next big running back. But look at these stats from last season."

Adam looked down at the page. "What about them?" he asked.

"Don't you see?" Noah asked. He finally looked up from his article and gazed at Adam. "In late-season games against strong defense, he falls apart," Noah explained. "He'll never make it in the pros. There's no way."

Adam frowned. "You think you know better than this writer does?" he asked. "And all those pro scouts?"

"You can quote me," Noah replied. Then he went back to reading his article.

A few moments later, a shadow fell over the magazine. Noah frowned. He was about to shout, "Get out of my light!" But then Eric Floyd, the first-string running back, came tumbling into him, followed by linemen from the other team.

Noah's magazine and stats notebook went flying.

He fell off the bench and tumbled into the first row of the bleachers. His head slammed into the muddy ground with a thud.

"Ugh," Noah said. He struggled to get up, but slipped in the mud and fell right on his face.

The crowds above him in the bleachers, all the cheerleaders, and everyone on his team roared with laughter.

Noah rolled onto his back and looked up at them. He was covered from head to toe in mud. Even the guys who had been in the game weren't as muddy as he was.

"Get up, Noah!" Coach French shouted. He came stomping over.

"Oh, man," Noah muttered.

"Where is your head?" the coach snapped. "When that play came close to the sideline, everyone else on the bench got out of the way."

"They did?" Noah said. He got to his feet and wiped the mud off his face.

The coach handed him a towel. "Even Adam got out of the way," Coach French said. "And he was right next to you!"

"Sorry, Coach," Noah said. He wiped his face and hands with the towel.

Adam strolled over, smiling. "I tried to warn you, Noah," Adam said. "I guess you didn't hear me shouting at you."

"I guess not," Noah admitted.

"And you probably don't remember me tugging at your sleeve?" Adam said with a smirk.

"No," Noah said, gritting his teeth, "I don't remember that either."

The coach shook his head slowly. He was obviously disappointed in Noah, and Adam wasn't helping the situation at all.

"Just go hit the showers," the coach said. "It looks like you won't be getting any game time today. We'll talk after the game."

CHAPTER 2

ON THE FIELD

After the game, Noah headed into the coach's office. The Wildcats had won, and they were celebrating in the locker room, but Noah knew he didn't get to take part in the celebration.

"Noah, you have to keep your nose out of those magazines and that stat book of yours," the coach said. He closed the door behind Noah and then sat down at his big metal desk. Noah sat across from him in a little plastic chair. His hair was still wet from the shower.

"You have to keep your eyes on the game," the coach went on.

"I'm sorry, Coach," Noah said. "The thing is, I just love football so much. Sometimes I get caught up in an article. Have you heard about Jack Tyler? See, everyone thinks —"

Coach French cut him off. "Yes, I've heard about Jack Tyler and I know what people think of him," the coach said. "But that really doesn't matter, not when we're in the middle of a game against the Bloomfield Buccaneers."

"But, Coach," Noah said. "I hardly ever play. What's the difference if I'm not always paying super-close attention?"

The coach shook his head. "Even on the bench you're an important part of the team," he said. "Did you see that handoff to Eric?"

"No," Noah said.

"Did you see the mistakes the line made?" the coach went on. "Did you see the misstep Carlos took after the snap?"

Noah shook his head. "No, Coach," he said. "I missed the whole play." He lowered his head and added, "Except when Eric dove on top of me. I saw that part."

"A player like you can be a great part of this team," Coach French said. "You've got a great head for the sport. If you had been paying attention during that play, your knowledge of football would have been helpful to Eric, Carlos, and the whole offensive line."

"Thanks, Coach. I guess I didn't see it like that," Noah said.

The coach grunted. "Just pay attention," he said. "You're not much help if your nose is always in a magazine. On paper, those stats are meaningless. It's on the field that they count."

"Got it, Coach," Noah said quietly.

CHAPTER 3

NOT
WORRIED

That night after dinner, Noah headed up to his room.

"Are you doing your homework up there?" Noah's dad called up the steps a couple of hours later.

It was almost eight, and Noah's school books sat unopened on his desk. Noah glanced at them, then back at the screen of his laptop.

"Um, yes, Dad," Noah called back.

But he wasn't doing his homework. He was looking at the website for his fantasy football league.

With Noah's love of football stats, his team was having a great season. Suddenly his computer dinged.

It was an instant message from Adam. Noah and Adam had become good friends during the season because they sat on the bench together for most of every game.

ADAMINATOR: Noah, you there?

NOAHPOTOMUS: Hey, Adam. Just looking at the fantasy football scores. Your team isn't doing so well.

ADAMINATOR: Yeah, yeah. Tell me about your meeting with the coach. Did he scream at you or what?

NOAHPOTOMUS: He was angry, but I'm not worried.

ADAMINATOR: You're not? Don't you remember last year? Coach French kicked those two eighth-graders off the team for leaving the field during a game.

NOAHPOTOMUS: They went to get hot dogs! I was reading about football.

There was a knock at Noah's door. "Just a minute, Dad," Noah called.

NOAHPOTOMUS: Hey, I have to go. But remember, I haven't played more than two minutes in one game all season. What difference does it make?

"Noah, open this door!" his dad said from the hall.

"Just a second, Dad!" Noah called.

NOAHPOTOMUS: Oh, one more thing. Did you see the fantasy football scores? My team is still undefeated!

ADAMINATOR: I'm not surprised. I'll see you tomorrow.

NOAHPOTOMUS: Bye.

Noah slammed his laptop closed. Then he opened all his schoolbooks and jumped up to open the door for his dad.

"Hi, Dad," he said. "What's up? I'm working hard in here. I was just finishing a math problem."

His dad looked around. "Yeah, I can see you're working hard," he said. He frowned, but then his face relaxed. "All right, kiddo," he said. "Let me know if you need any help. I'll be downstairs."

CHAPTER 4

FAMOUS
TOUCHDOWNS

"Check this out," Noah said to Adam as they walked to the field before practice started the next afternoon. He held out a magazine that looked older than either of them. It was sealed inside a clear plastic bag, like the ones Adam's older brother used to store his comic collection.

"What are you showing me?" Adam asked.

"This is a special magazine about the 1967 NFL Championship between Dallas and Green Bay," Noah said. "You have to check this out. It was one of the best and most famous games in the history of football!"

The two boys sat on the front row of the bleachers. Noah read through the magazine while they waited for the rest of the team.

"Look at this," Noah said. He pointed at a full-spread photo of a touchdown.

It looked like nearly every player from both teams was piled in a heap on the goal line. In the front of the photo, an official, wearing his striped black-and-white jersey, had both of his arms straight up, signaling a touchdown.

"What's the big deal about this picture?" Adam asked.

"This is one of the most famous touchdowns in football history," Noah explained. "Not only did it win the game for Green Bay, it also —"

A whistle blew close to Noah's ear. He jumped and almost dropped his magazine.

"Ow!" he said, turning toward the sound of the whistle.

Coach French stood next to him, glaring down at Noah.

"Um, hi, Coach," Noah stammered. Then he looked around.

The Ice Bowl is considered to be one of the best games of football ever played! This is mainly due to the intensity of the weather, the rivalry between the two teams, how important the game was, and the intense conclusion to the game.

The rest of the team was already gathered on the field, waiting for practice to start. Noah hadn't even noticed that Adam wasn't sitting next to him anymore.

"Um, sorry," Noah said.

He slipped his magazine back into its plastic bag. "I got caught up in this story about the 1967 NFL Championship," Noah went on.

"Yeah, I noticed," Coach French said, raising an eyebrow.

"Green Bay ran a sneak to win the game, Coach," Noah said. He put the magazine down and got up to join the others. "Even the coach didn't think it would work. But it did."

"Yes, I remember reading about that game," the coach replied. He put a hand on Noah's shoulder and guided him toward the other players on the sideline.

"Maybe we could use a sneak in the game against the Eagles next week?" Noah said. He pulled on his helmet.

"Thanks for the tip, Noah," the coach said. "But let's just run the plays we actually know."

He patted Noah on the helmet. Then he blew his whistle again and started going over the plays for the game against the Eagles.

Noah knew every play his team ran — and most other teams ran — by heart. He didn't need to listen to the coach repeating them. Before too long, his mind was wandering.

Noah didn't even realize that his coach was noticing.

CHAPTER 5

ON THE BENCH

The game against the Eagles was the following Thursday. Noah knew he wouldn't play much, if at all.

He sat on the bench with his helmet between his feet. His stats notebook was on the bench next to him, between him and Adam.

"It's cold today," Adam said. He blew into his hands.

Noah nodded. "The news said it'll get down to freezing overnight," he said.

"I wish I were playing," Adam said. "Then I'd stay warm!"

Noah said, "There's no chance I'll play today. Coach is mad at me." He shrugged. "I don't know what to do about it. I can't just stop loving stats and football history."

He watched the game carefully, and noted every stat he could think of in his notebook.

"What are you writing down in your book?" Adam asked.

"I'm keeping track of gains, what plays are working, tackles, sacks, completions . . ." Noah said. "You name it, I'm writing it down."

Adam shook his head. "Didn't Coach French tell you to keep your head out of your stats book?" he asked.

"I'm keeping stats on this game," Noah said. "That means not only do I get to record stats and go through my notebook, but I end up paying close attention to the team and the game, too. This should make everyone happy."

The boys both looked up at the field as their quarterback, Carlos Suarez, took a long snap.

Carlos spun to his right, then cut left and handed off to Eric, the first-string running back.

Eric cut back to the right and then turned up field. He spun once to get through the defensive line, and then put his head down and started toward the end zone.

It was not a clear run, though. An Eagles defensive back was too fast even for Eric. Before anyone knew what was happening, the defensive back was on top of Eric in an instant.

Eric tried to dodge, but he cut right into his blocker and they both went down. The Eagles back jumped on both of them and the whistle blew.

"Ow!" Eric screamed from the bottom of the pile-up. "My ankle!"

The whistle blew again as the Eagles defensive back and the Wildcats fullback got to their feet. The medics and Coach French quickly ran out to the field.

Noah and Adam watched from the bench. It looked like Eric was really hurt.

"That looks bad," Adam said quietly.

Noah nodded. He was too shaken to even write down the stats of the play.

The coach and the medics crouched over Eric's ankle. Now and then, Noah could hear Eric yell out in pain.

After a few minutes, one of the medics ran to their truck. He came back carrying a stretcher.

"Oh no," Adam said. "Looks like Eric is coming out of the game."

Noah nodded. "That's too bad. I bet he sprained his ankle," he said. "I hope it doesn't ruin the rest of his season. Let's just hope it wasn't a broken bone."

Adam shuddered. "That would be awful," he said. "I hope he's okay."

The fans and other Wildcats clapped for Eric as he was carried off the field.

Noah grabbed his pen and his stats book. He marked down the eight yards Eric had gained on the lead run, the play they'd just done. Then he marked that Eric had been injured and had to leave the game.

Noah looked up as Eric was loaded onto the stretcher. Coach French was heading in his direction, carrying Eric's helmet.

Noah looked back at his notebook and marked that the second-string running back would be entering the game.

Then he realized he was marking his own row in the stat book.

The second-string running back was him.

CHAPTER 6

YOU'RE IN

"You're in, Noah," Coach French said, patting him on the shoulder.

"Um, okay," Noah said nervously. "You got it, Coach."

Noah pulled on his helmet and jogged out to the huddle. He passed the two medics who were carrying Eric off the field.

Eric held up his hand as he went past. Noah gave him a high five.

"Good luck," Eric said.

"Thanks," Noah said. "I hope your ankle is okay."

Noah ran onto the field and joined the huddle. It was cold. His breath came out from his helmet like a puff of smoke. The whole huddle was full of clouds from the players breathing.

"Noah, we're going straight to you," Carlos said. Noah could see him smirking behind his facemask. "I hope you're feeling warmed up," Carlos went on. "Okay, on three, run counter."

Noah nodded. The play meant Carlos would try to get the defense off Noah with a fake. If it worked, Noah could run in open field. If it didn't, Noah would be pretty much alone, with no blockers.

Carlos clapped and shouted, "Break!" The team got lined up in shotgun position. Carlos barked at the center: "Hut, hut, hut!"

The center snapped the football. Carlos caught the ball and faded back to the left. The defensive line moved with him. Noah ran to the left too, to take the handoff. As he ran, he spotted a defender on the Eagles line, number 66.

He remembered number 66 from his stats book. Number 66 never fell for the fake.

Carlos turned and gave Noah the handoff as Noah cut back to the right side. The defense should have been weaker, but Noah glanced at the Eagles' number 66.

What if number 66 wasn't fooled by the fake to the left?

Noah decided to cut back to the left, where the offensive line could protect him.

"Noah, weak side!" Carlos shouted, but it was too late.

Noah ran straight into the line, a mass of his own linemen and Eagles defensive linemen. The Wildcats linemen didn't expect Noah to come running up from behind them. They were confused and tried to make a path for him.

Instead they opened up and let the defenders rush through. They plowed into Noah, sending him flying deeper into the backfield and onto his back with a thud.

The whistle blew. Noah looked up at the sky. He watched his breath form a cloud over him for a second. It was bright white against the clear blue sky.

Carlos was standing over him. He reached out his hand to help Noah up, and Noah took it.

"Why'd you go left?" Carlos said.

Noah shook the tackle from his head and tried to reply. He heard the referee call out, "A loss of eight yards."

"There goes Eric's run," Carlos said. "And now it's third down." The quarterback shook his head and got into the huddle.

Noah followed him, hanging his head.

CHAPTER 7

BLOWN IT

Carlos looked hard at Noah in the huddle. "We're running again, Noah," he said. "Power sweep. Wait for your guards, okay?"

Noah knew the play well. It would get some good yardage if the guards picked up the defenders in time. Otherwise, Noah would end up running straight out of bounds — or getting pounded into the grass again.

Noah started running. He knew he couldn't cut up field until the defense had been fully sealed off. But his guards weren't big enough or strong enough to hold the defenders this time.

The defensive line pushed through, and the hole wasn't big enough to slip through. Noah and his guards were being forced straight toward the sideline.

No way, Noah thought. *I'm not letting another loss of yards show up in my stats.*

Noah cut back to the left. The defenders were fooled, just for a moment, and Noah cut up the field.

It wasn't enough, though. The rest of the defensive line had already recovered and closed up the hole.

Noah threw up his arm and held the ball in one hand, like he'd seen so many great running backs do, but it didn't make any difference.

In an instant, he found himself face first in the grass. There was a clump of dirt and turf stuck in his facemask.

"Ugh . . ." he groaned. He just wanted to stay where he was.

The Eagles who had taken him down got up and high-fived. Noah managed to get to his feet too, but he wasn't feeling as good as they were.

The ref called out, "Loss of five yards. Fourth down."

Carlos walked past Noah and pulled off his helmet. "I guess we're not scoring this half," he said. "Here comes the kicking team."

Noah looked at the bench. Their kicker and special teams were heading for the field. Noah had blown it.

CHAPTER 8

DO YOUR OWN THING

The Eagles scored a second field goal on their next and last drive of the half, making the score 6-0. Then, suddenly, it was halftime. Noah ran as fast as he could off the field and into the locker room, trying to stay warm.

Coach French led the halftime conference, going over plays and mistakes. With a couple of minutes left in halftime, he sent the boys back to the field.

Noah started walking out, but Coach French said, "Hold on a minute, Noah. I want to talk to you."

"What's up, Coach?" Noah asked. He tried to smile, but he knew the coach wanted to scold him for the mistakes he'd made in the first half.

"Noah, I don't know where your head is," the coach said. Noah looked down at the ground. "I thought you were just distracted when you were on the bench. You can't be looking at that stats book of yours while you're on the field."

"No, Coach," Noah said. "I'm not."

"Then what's wrong?" the coach asked, looking Noah in the eye. "You know those plays. Those are standard running plays — nothing fancy."

"Sure, I know them," Noah said. "I've run them a hundred times. And I've seen them run a thousand times or more."

"Then what happened out there?" the coach asked. "You went to the strong side on that first run, and on that second . . . well, you could have just run out of bounds and avoided getting plowed and the additional yard loss."

Noah took a deep breath. "The Eagles have a defender, number 66, who never falls for a fake."

"Number 66?" the coach said. "That's Lawrence Crenshaw. He's a good player."

"Right," Noah said. "When I saw him on the line, I remembered his stats against fakes. I had a feeling he'd catch me on the weak side and clobber me."

"But he did fall for it," the coach said. "The right was wide open. You could have made a great gain, at least to the secondary."

"The stats said he'd catch me," Noah said. "I went with the stats."

The coach sighed. "Okay, what about that sweep?" he asked. "No stats there. Your guards didn't shut down the D. You should have run to the sideline, cut your losses."

"I was watching some old games over the weekend," Noah said. "I saw this great run by Earl Campbell —"

"Earl Campbell?" Coach French repeated. Then he held his stomach and laughed. "I'm sorry, Noah," he went on, still laughing. "But Earl Campbell might be the greatest running back of all time."

"Exactly!" Noah said. "Shouldn't I learn from the best?"

The coach managed to stop laughing. He sat down next to Noah on the bench.

"Sure, you should learn from the best," Coach French said. "Really, Noah, it's terrific that you follow the greats and know so much about the sport. Lots of guys on the team have no idea about the history of football."

"Well, I'm trying," Noah said.

"Earl Campbell could get through any line, Noah," the coach said. "He was like a truck. You're . . . well, sorry, kid, but you're just not."

Noah sighed. "I know," he said. "But I have to play to my strengths, right? And my strengths are knowing the great players and the great plays!"

"That doesn't mean you just try to be them," the coach replied. "It means you learn from them and try to apply those lessons to your own playing."

"What about stats?" Noah asked. "If I know number 66 on the Eagles is tough to fake, shouldn't I try something other than a fake?"

"Not necessarily," the coach said. "Maybe it just means you keep an eye on him during play-action or that you should let the team know that number 66 is a sneaky player."

"I guess," Noah said. "I think I'm starting to get what you're saying."

The coach got up and put a hand on Noah's shoulder. "Let's get back out there," he said. "Just remember, sometimes it's a good idea to stick to what you know how to do. Forget what you know others have done. Do your own thing."

Coach French walked out of the locker room. Slowly, Noah stood up and followed him.

CHAPTER 9

SECOND HALF

The second half felt very long to Noah. Coach French and Carlos focused on the passing game. Though they made some good gains, Noah's only role was to pretend to take a handoff now and then for a play-action pass. Carlos called pass after pass.

Andrew Tucker made a few receptions, but it wasn't enough. As the end of the fourth quarter got closer, the Wildcats had only scored one field goal. Their defense had been good, so the Eagles hadn't scored again. But that meant the score was still 6-3.

At the two-minute warning, it was third down. The Wildcats would need a field goal to tie and a touchdown to win.

"Just get us a few yards," Coach French said to Carlos. "We need to get into field goal range. Then we can win in overtime."

Carlos nodded as the official called for the teams to take the field again.

"They'll be expecting a run," the coach said. "So, Andrew, stop after about eight steps, and Carlos, just connect. Then our kicker will make the three."

The offense took the field. When they were lined up, Noah looked out over the defense.

Something wasn't right, he noticed. The defensive line was stacked.

"Carlos," Noah said from the back. "Hey, Carlos, listen to me."

Carlos looked over his shoulder. "What's up?" he asked.

"They're rushing," Noah said. "They want to force us into fourth down with a loss and no options. Call blue 19."

"A toss sweep?" Carlos said. "That's crazy. They wouldn't risk taking their whole D out of the game. They know we can go long if they do. Besides, you can't outrun this defensive line."

"I won't have to," Noah said. "They'll only have two players who aren't on top of you by the time I start running!"

Carlos shook his head and started the count, but he glanced at the coach. Andrew started his jog across the backfield.

Noah stood up and called over to the sideline. "Coach!" Noah said.

Coach French looked at him, and Noah pointed to the defensive line, then at the cornerbacks. They looked ready to pounce.

The coach nodded, and then called out to Carlos. "Blue 19," Coach French said.

Carlos stopped the count and stood up straight. Then he stepped back into shotgun position and started the count again.

"Blue, 19," Carlos barked. "Blue, 19. Hut!"

The center snapped the ball and Noah cut hard to the left.

Carlos immediately tossed the ball to Noah, just as the entire defensive line crashed through the Wildcats line. A moment later, they fell onto Carlos, but they were too late.

Noah had the ball. He ran as fast as he could up the sideline. He easily got ten yards for the first down, and the end zone was in sight.

Noah gave everything he had in every step. He could hear the breath and footsteps of the Eagles safety behind him.

The safety grunted and Noah felt arms wrap around his knees. His feet gave out just as he reached the goal line, but he held on to the ball and collapsed into the end zone.

Noah rolled onto his back in time to see the official throw up both his arms.

"Touchdown!" the official yelled.

The rest of the offense came running up the field. Carlos pulled off his helmet as he ran.

"That was amazing!" Carlos shouted.

"Great run!" Andrew said.

After a brief celebration in the end zone and the extra point kick, the score was 10-6, Wildcats.

Noah clapped for the defense as they took the field. Coach French walked over to Noah.

"Great job, Noah," the coach said. "That was a great call."

"Thanks, Coach," Noah replied.

"Do you know why that play went so well?" the coach asked.

Noah nodded. "Sure," he said. "I ran like Earl Campbell." He smiled. "Not really. But I played up my strengths."

Adam overheard the conversation and walked over. "What do you mean?" he asked. "How did you play up your strengths?"

"Well," Noah replied, "I saw how the defense lined up. I knew they would be trying anything to stop us from getting that first down."

"And you know that because of your expertise with stats, football history, and smart plays," Coach French added.

"And since I know all our plays so well," Noah said, "I was able to tell Carlos what a good play to call would be."

"You called that?" Adam asked.
"I thought Carlos did!"

Noah laughed. "Before I got Coach French's
attention," he said, "Carlos thought I was crazy!"

Carlos put his arm around Noah's
shoulder. "I still think you're crazy," Carlos
said, smiling. "But now I know it's worth it!"